MW01141268

The Rooster Who Loved the Violin

by Ben Harrison

illustrations by Carrie Disrud

Whirlygig Kids Books
An Imprint of Absolutely Amazing eBooks

ISBN-13: 978-1508463979

ISBN-10:1508463972

Dedicated to Helen's and my grandson, Roman, who, at six-years-old, already loves books and is always adding to his collection. Hopefully, this is only the beginning of a long relationship with the printed word.

I will never forget my first favorite book—*The Little Airplane*, about Pilot Small, who had to make an emergency landing in his airplane to repair a fuel line before he could continue on to his destination. It is the story of a person having to deal with and overcome adversity.

The Rooster Who Loved the Violin is also dedicated to our two sons, Benjamin and Cole.

The Rooster who Loved the Violin

By Ben Harrison

illustrations By Carrie Disrud

There ONCE WAS a MaN named GiNO

Who playeD thE violin At a RestaurANte Italiano Where GiNo playeD FoR his FrieNds

His Music was so lovely it Always maDe People SmiLE, LoVers would hold each Other's HanDs And LooK inTo each other's eyes

Then From out OF NO Where a terrible problem AROse

WhaT was the Solution? NoBody seemED to Know A Big Red Rooster Mr. Cock-a-DooDle-DO Flew inTo A large tree next To GiNo's Dining Room

PrOBlem ? = SoLUTiON

He was A
Goofy
Rooster as
Far as roosters
Go, He loveD to
hear GiNO's
violiN and
WAtch Him play
with His
Bow

BUT! the Rooster
CrOweD at LoVe SONgs
He CrOweD At the
MoOn GiNo CoUld
Not play His Violin
when he COCK-a-
DoOdle-dooD !

BaCK to the FARM

PiG

HORSE

HEN

CaT

DOG

ROOSTER
?

He Was A FrienDly rooSteR
GinO meant him NO Harm
He just wanted To CatCH HiM
Take Him **BaCK to The FaRm**

But the Rooster
was Quite crafty
And He Did Not
UnderStanD
EverytimE GiNo
chaseD him He
Flew anD hE
Ran

6
6
BUY A NeT!!!
ThE Next niGht At tHe Restaurante when againN Gino could not play HE wondered OUTLoud,
"WhaT should i Do To Make the Rooster go Away?"
THen he thougHt, "I've got An iDea I'll GO
BUY A Net
I'll sneak up behiNd the Rooster AnD I'll cAtch him, I'll Bet!"
6
6

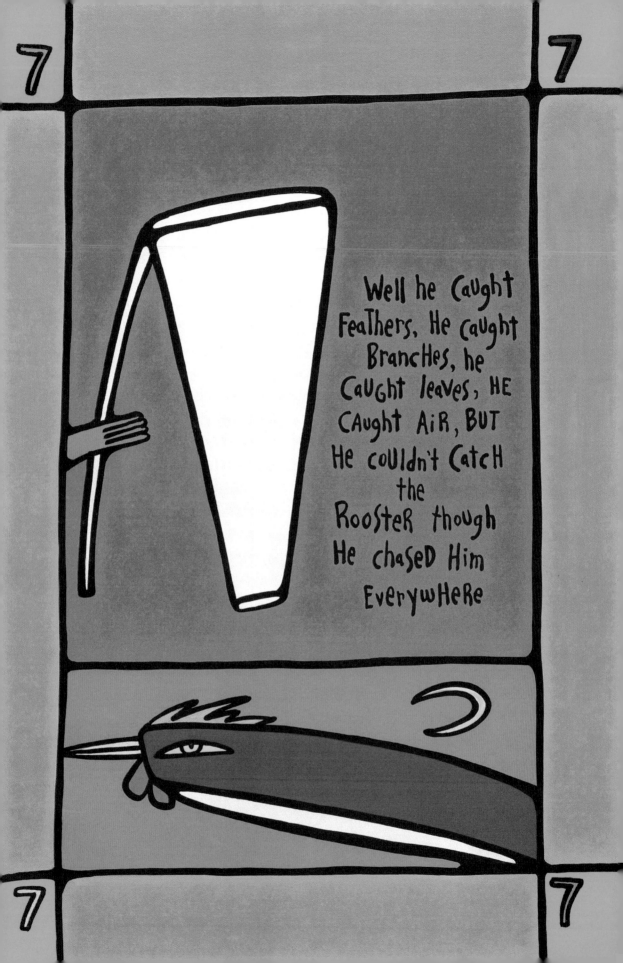

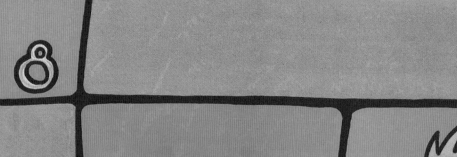

FiNally, hE called FaRmer Cole He'd Know what To DO Surely FaRmer CoIE coUId cAtch COCK-a Doodle - DO

FaRmeR Cole pulled up in the DriVewAy In HiS straw CoVereD PICK-up TrUcK AND in The BaCK wAs a Beautiful Hen who softly clucKeD AnD ShE clucKed

WHeN the ReD RoOSTeR SAW HeR he FleW DoWN neXT to the HeN all the way bACK to THe FaRm HE tRieD to cRoW LiKe A VioLiN

SooN there were eggs iN the HeN house, SooN theRe weRe EggS iN THE BaRn... THeN little chicks Everywhere ON FaRmer Cole's FaRm

THeN

PEACE AND QUIET

Now the moral of this story the lesson to be learned from it all, if you play the violin and a rooster joins in don't run around like a chicken to catch him call Farmer Cole and a hen.

Key West Chickens

by Ben Harrison

I wrote the make-believe story about The Rooster Who Loved the Violin after a real rooster came to our family home and decided he wanted to nest in a tree in our front yard.

We live on the corner of White and Olivia Streets, in Key West, Florida, in an old two-story, wood-framed house with three bedrooms and a balcony upstairs. It overlooks White Street, which runs all the way from the Gulf of Mexico to the Caribbean Sea—approximately a mile from seashore to seashore.

The house was built about 100 years ago, before air conditioning, so to make the rooms cooler (heat rises) the ceilings are high and the house is tall. Next door is our workshop/art gallery, Harrison Gallery, so we don't have very far to go to work.

It was around five o'clock in the morning when our rooster first let us know he was moving in. Startled awake by a loud cock-a-doodle-doo that could easily be heard a block away, he must have wanted us to get up early and go to work like farmer Cole does every morning.

After the third and fourth cock-a-doodle-doo, I got out of bed, put a towel around my waist and went outside to try and find out where he was hiding. His voice was so loud I could see lights going on in other nearby homes.

He was a smart rooster because, as soon as I started looking for him, he didn't make a peep. But when I got back into bed, another cock-a-doodle-doo made me try to find him again.

I could tell from the sound that he was close to our son's bedroom. With the towel back around my waist, I got a flashlight and went out on the balcony to look and see if he was in the tall sea hibiscus tree.

Sure enough, there he was perched 25-feet above the ground in the branches. The only thing I could do if we wanted to go back to sleep was somehow get him out of the tree and make him go down the block to the Harvey Government Center on the corner of White and Truman Streets, where all of his fellow chickens roost.

I didn't want to hurt him, but he, like The Rooster Who Loved the Violin, needed to go back among his friends who sleep in the two large trees there. Chickens here in Key West have plenty of friends. There are between two and three-thousand of them strutting around this small island.

Across the street from the government center is Dion's Quik Chik, that sells the best fried chicken in town. Fowl like to hang out there, too. Though you would think it might make them a little nervous, they're not.

Like all of the birds in Key West, it is against the law to harm them and they seem to know this. On the other corner of the intersection is the White Street Chevron gas station where several chicken families roam the nearby alleyways, scratching around for food.

Further up White Street is Sandy's Cafe where there are outdoor stools next to painted red countertops. While people eat their bacon, egg and cheese sandwiches or Cuban Mix sandwiches along with aromatic Cuban coffee, you can see them walking around people's feet, waiting for a handout or for crumbs to fall.

Now that I had found the rooster in the tree, I had an idea that I thought would be the answer to my problem.

I went downstairs and got our garden hose. Lifting it from the front porch to the upstairs balcony wasn't easy, but I got the hose nozzle hooked on the railing.

From there I climbed the stairs to the balcony and got the hose. With the flashlight in one hand and the hose in the other, I started squirting the big bird.

He didn't care! He just looked at me, "Squirt me all you want. I live in the rain. I've lived through a hurricane."

He didn't budge.

Then I had another idea.

We have a long plastic pole with a basket on one end that we use to pick ripe mangos and avocados from our local fruit trees. There's a big mango tree on White Street that can bear hundreds, and they all ripen at about the same time. You don't want them to squish falling off of the tree onto the ground, especially one this large.

I was hoping I could coax him down with the basket on the end of the pole.

Darn... it wasn't long enough. I'd have to get our tall ladder.

With a towel still around my waist, on top of the ladder, I could just barely reach him.

He hadn't minded the water, but he didn't like being touched. Thrashing, he scared me as he flew over my head to the sidewalk below.

Under the street light I could see he had turquoise tail feathers, a red comb on top his head, with yellow and yellowish-brown feathers on his body that shined in the glow of the street lamp. He was a proud rooster. I could tell by the way he held his head.

In Key West, most people love these colorful birds that were brought here by settlers from Cuba.

One rooster used to come into a local judge's living room and sit on his lap while he watched the evening news. The judge lives in Bahama Village, another part of town they love. It's called "Bahama Village" because that is where settlers from the Bahama Islands chose to live.

Close to the judge's home is the Blue Heaven Restaurant where they roam in between the tables underneath a banyan tree that once shaded Key West's most famous author, Ernest Hemingway.

My rooster was mad. I could tell by the look in his green eye with a black pupil that as soon as I got back into bed, he was going to fly right back to that tree where he had decided he wanted to live. I put the mango picker down and picked up the broom I use to sweep the front sidewalk. Still holding the towel so it wouldn't fall off, I began chasing him down the street.

People talk about herding cats and how hard that is. Cats are easy compared to chickens. He darted in and around the cars parked on Olivia Street, which runs by the side of our house. In front of the former Catholic monastery that had been converted into a house by the owners of the Red Rooster Inn, he ducked into the driveway, then doubled back.

I had to be quick and I had to hold on to the broom and the towel at the same time. He got behind me once making me go to the other side of the street so I could sneak up on him again. He darted this way and that so I had to do the same thing.

It was summer and the few tourists here were still in bed.

The drivers of the cars that passed me in the early hours of the morning didn't even bother looking twice to see what I was doing. They knew that I was just a guy who couldn't sleep, holding a towel around his waist as he chased a rooster with a broom.

There are even chickens on Duval Street, our main street. One rooster, on a Sunday morning walked down the isle of St. Paul's Episcopal Church during the church service. The church is not far from the post office and county courthouse where they live in abundance.

The roosters are the loud ones that crow and are answered by other roosters, sometimes blocks away.

The hens cluck quietly as they teach their little chicks how to scratch in the dirt for food.

One day, walking down White Street on my way to Fausto's Food Palace, the local grocery store where I shop, I once saw a big man with big muscles bulging out of his tank top stop his car in the middle of the road to hold up traffic while he helped a hen and her ten baby chicks cross the road. It was a tender moment.

The little chicks always stay close to their mother.

The rooster I chased back to his previous home must have learned his lesson because he never bothered us again.

I play the guitar and even wrote a song about roosters. I also know a song about a boy who raised a hog as though he were a dog. But that's another story for another day.

Other works by Ben Harrison:

Ben's website is benharrisonkeywest.com and he can be reached by email at benharrisonkw@gmail.com.

The website for Harrison Gallery is harrison-gallery.com, and you can visit in person at 825 White Street, Key West, FL 33040.

Books:

SAILING DOWN THE MOUNTAIN: A COSTA RICAN ADVENTURE
A delightful book that will appeal not only to those interested in sailing, but to anyone who's ever tasted wanderlust or dreamt of breaking free from 'normal' life and doing something truly extraordinary. Harrison blends journal entries, unique historical commentary, song lyrics, personal photos, and more in his adventure autobiography of a couple in the 1970s who make it through challenging and oftentimes hilarious odds. Quirky, heartfelt, and fun, Sailing Down the Mountain is a must-read that transcends generations. Absolutely Amazing eBooks/The New Atlantian Library

UNDYING LOVE
A darkly humorous non-fiction book about the bizarre Count Carl Von Cosel and his unearthly love for the beautiful, but terminally ill, Maria Elena Hoyos. It takes place during the 1930s in Key West. Absolutely Amazing eBooks & Ketch and Yawl Publishing (trade paperback)

CHARLIE JONES
From California to Corpus Christi, Texas, and Mexico, this fast-paced generational novel follows different characters as they navigate life, parenting, art and money. Often funny and at times emotional, it's a racy and entertaining ride through their lives. Absolutely Amazing eBooks/The New Atlantian Library

OFFICIAL VISIT
A book about college and professional baseball recruiting, which Ben and his son went through.
Author House (trade paperback)

All of Ben's books can be purchased on Amazon.

Albums:

KEY WEST, A MUSICAL TOUR ABOUT TOWN
Chronicles the foibles of the characters, past and present, of the quirky island of Key West.

DUVAL YEARS
A three CD collection of music written and recorded during Ben's years as a regular performer on Key West's famed Duval Street.

ERIN ELKINS and BEN HARRISON
Ben shares the vocals on these original country/jazzy compositions with Erin Elkins, a Key West girl currently performing in New York City.

AIR SUNSHINE
A musical journey back to the time in Key West when "there were five digit phone numbers, dogs without leashes, bars without TVs, and silver airplanes in the clear blue sky." Included is a song about Bettie Page, who lived in Key West for two years.

Ben's music can be bought on Amazon, iTunes, and CD Baby.

Musicals:

KEY WEST, A MUSICAL TOUR ABOUT TOWN

UNDYING LOVE
(book and music by Ben Harrison)

CLOUDS OVER THE SUNSHINE INN
About a fictional chain of hotels that cater to the health-conscious traveler— a comedic parable about getting your just desserts.
(book by Ben Harrison and Richard Grusin, music by Ben Harrison)

AbsolutelyAmazingEbooks.com

or

AA-eBooks.com

49982317R00031

Made in the USA
Charleston, SC
13 December 2015